A VERY SQUEAKY MYSTERY

Written by Laura Angelina & Randy Williamson

Illustrations by Laura Angelina

Published in 2015 by RainbowLeaf Books.

Text copyright © 2014 Laura Angelina & Randy Williamson
Illustrations copyright © 2014 Laura Angelina

All rights reserved. No portion of this book may be reproduced, stored in a retrieval system, or transmitted in any form or by any means, mechanical, electronic, photocopying, recording, or otherwise without written permission from the publisher.

ISBN: 978-0-9891888-0-7 (Hardcover)
ISBN: 978-0-9891888-1-4 (Softcover)

Library of Congress Control Number: 2014951557

The illustrations for this book were created using digital media, watercolors and acrylic, pen and pencil.

Reinforced binding

Printed in China

1106 2nd Avenue South
Tierra Verde, Florida 33715
United States of America
www.rainbowleafbooks.com

For you, my brother, and all gentle souls.

They have breakfast in the morning, lunch later in the day, and dinner at night. But what they love the most is a peanut butter and jelly sandwich snack at four o'clock.

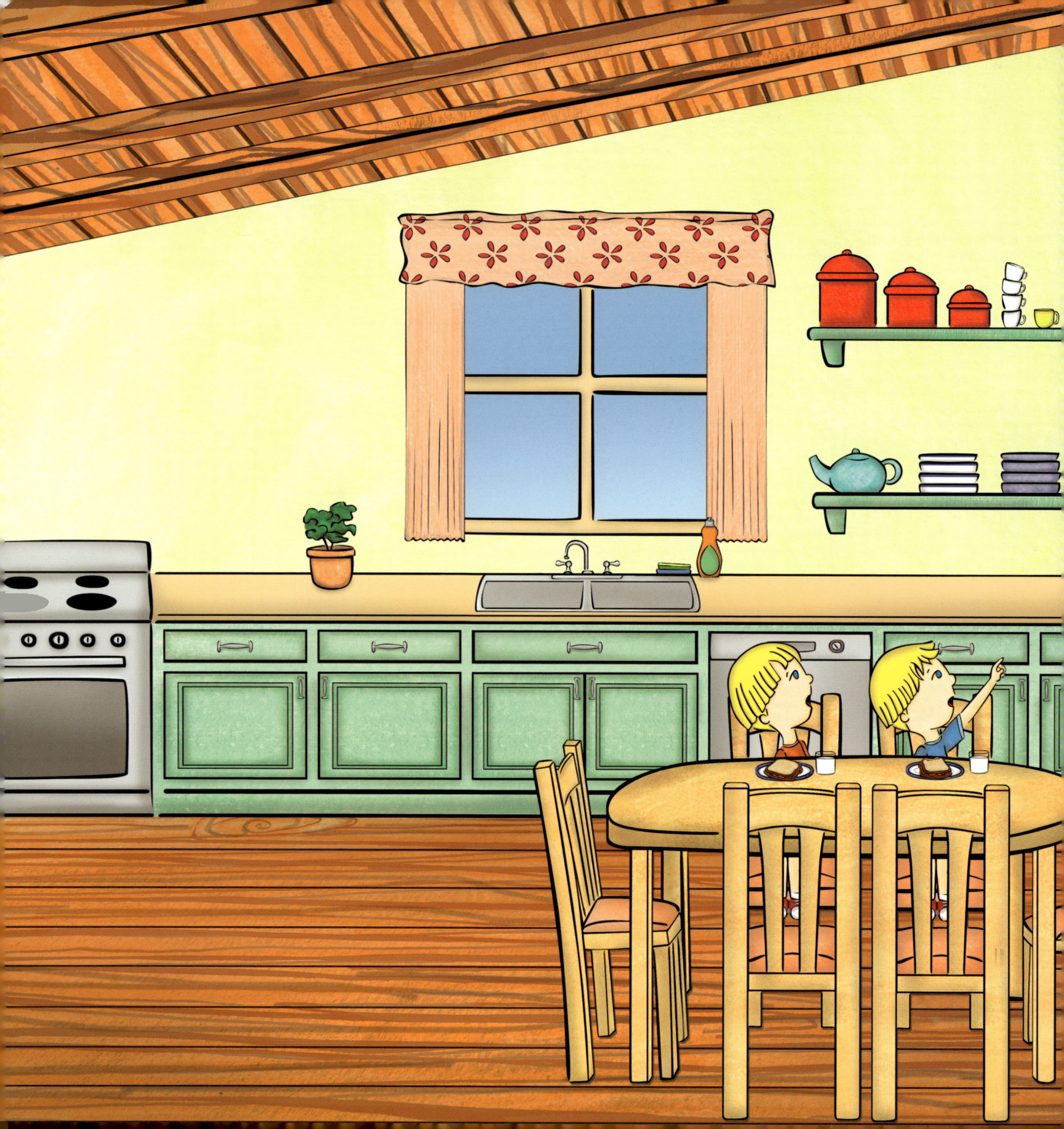

"What was that?" asked Kevin.

"Did you hear it too?" Scott replied.

"Yes, I did," answered Kevin.

"I wonder what could be making that squeaky noise."

"I know!" said Scott. "It could be a mouse! We should catch him!"

"I agree," said Kevin. "And I think I have an idea. Let's leave a piece of cheese out in the kitchen. Later tonight, the mouse might come out to eat it. We will be there and ready to catch him faster than you can say, 'Squeak.'"

After their parents tucked them in bed for the night, the twins pretended they had fallen asleep. But Kevin and Scott kept peeking until they were sure that the "coast was clear."

Everything was very quiet in the cabin. Without making a sound, the twins tiptoed on their way to the kitchen.

After cutting a piece of cheese and placing it on a plate on the table, Kevin and Scott hid behind a wall. The twins waited and waited, but the mouse did not show up. It was getting late, and they were really sleepy so they decided to give up for the night and go back to bed.

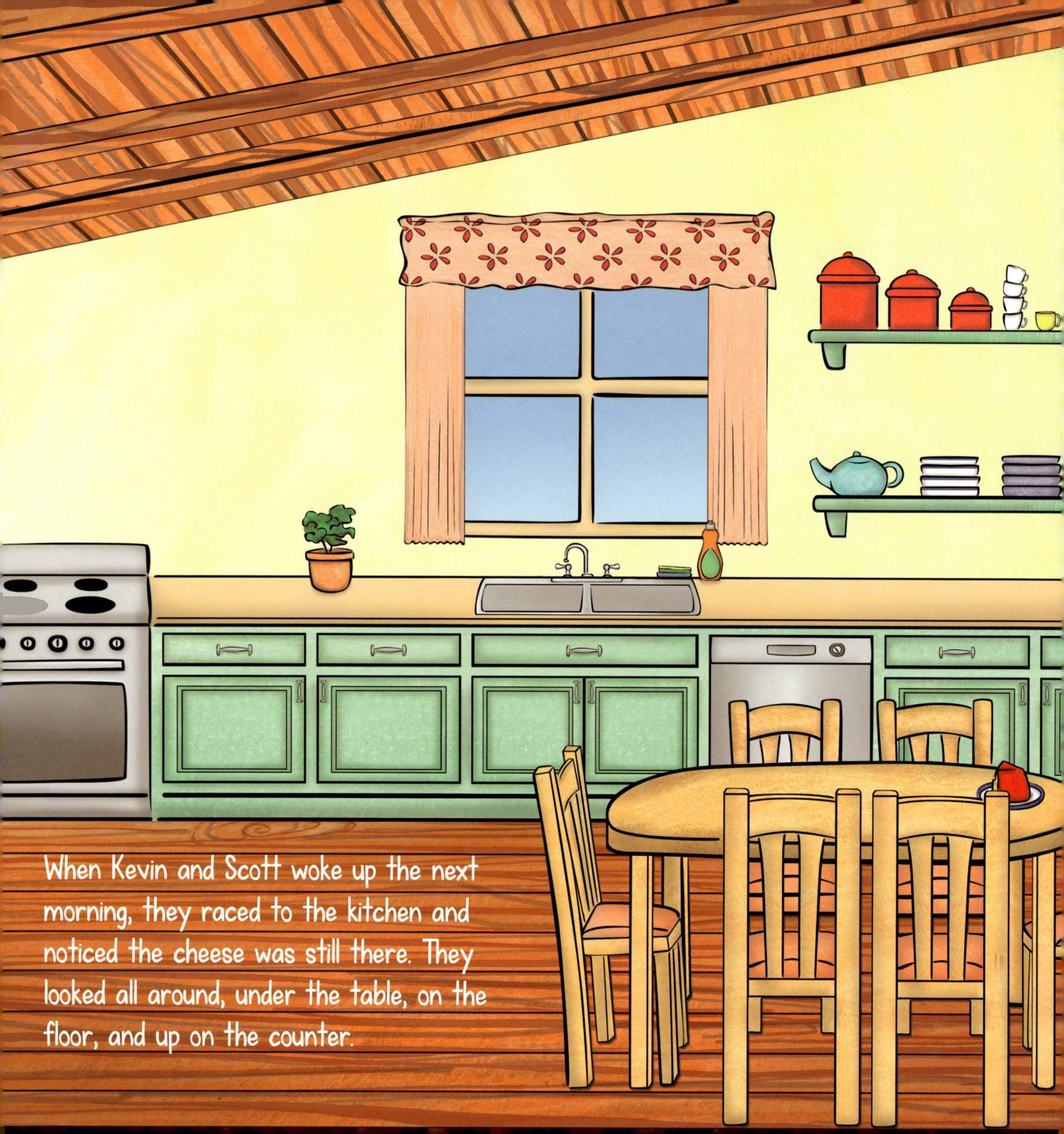

When Kevin and Scott woke up the next morning, they raced to the kitchen and noticed the cheese was still there. They looked all around, under the table, on the floor, and up on the counter.

At four o'clock, the twins opened the pantry to prepare their usual snack and quickly realized that the peanut butter was gone! They were surprised to hear, "Squeak, squeak, squeak, squeak."

"What was that?" asked Kevin.

"You heard it again?" Scott replied.

"Yes, I did," answered Kevin. "But now, I don't think it's a mouse, because he didn't eat the cheese. I wonder what it really is."

"Oh, I know!" said Scott. "It's probably a bat! So, what's our next plan?"

"Well, if it's really a bat, it's gonna come out only when it's really, really dark to eat bugs. That's when we can catch him!" said Kevin.

"Yeah!" Scott agreed.

Late that night, the twins once again pretended they had fallen asleep. In the middle of the night, they tiptoed to the kitchen, turned off all the lights, and waited for the bat to come out.

Several hours later, the twins were just about to give up when they heard, "Squeak, squeak, squeak, squeak."

Bam! Kevin and Scott rushed to catch the bat. Because it was so dark, they couldn't see a thing and accidentally bumped into each other's head. Dizzy and tired, they went back to bed.

The next day, they opened the refrigerator.
This time, the jelly was gone!

Sounding like a detective, Kevin said, "Indeed, this is a mystery."

"First the peanut butter and now the jelly!" Scott added.

"Hmm, if it's not a bat," said Kevin, "what possible squeaky thing could it be?"

"Aha! I know what it is!" Scott yelled. "It must be a peanut butter and jelly sandwich eating monster!"

"Yeah! That's probably it!" Kevin agreed. "He's been very lucky so far and already has the peanut butter and the jelly. But when he comes tonight looking for the bread, we will be prepared to catch him!"

Once again, the twins went to the kitchen in the middle of the night. But this time, they carried flashlights and used pots and pans as their armor against the monster.

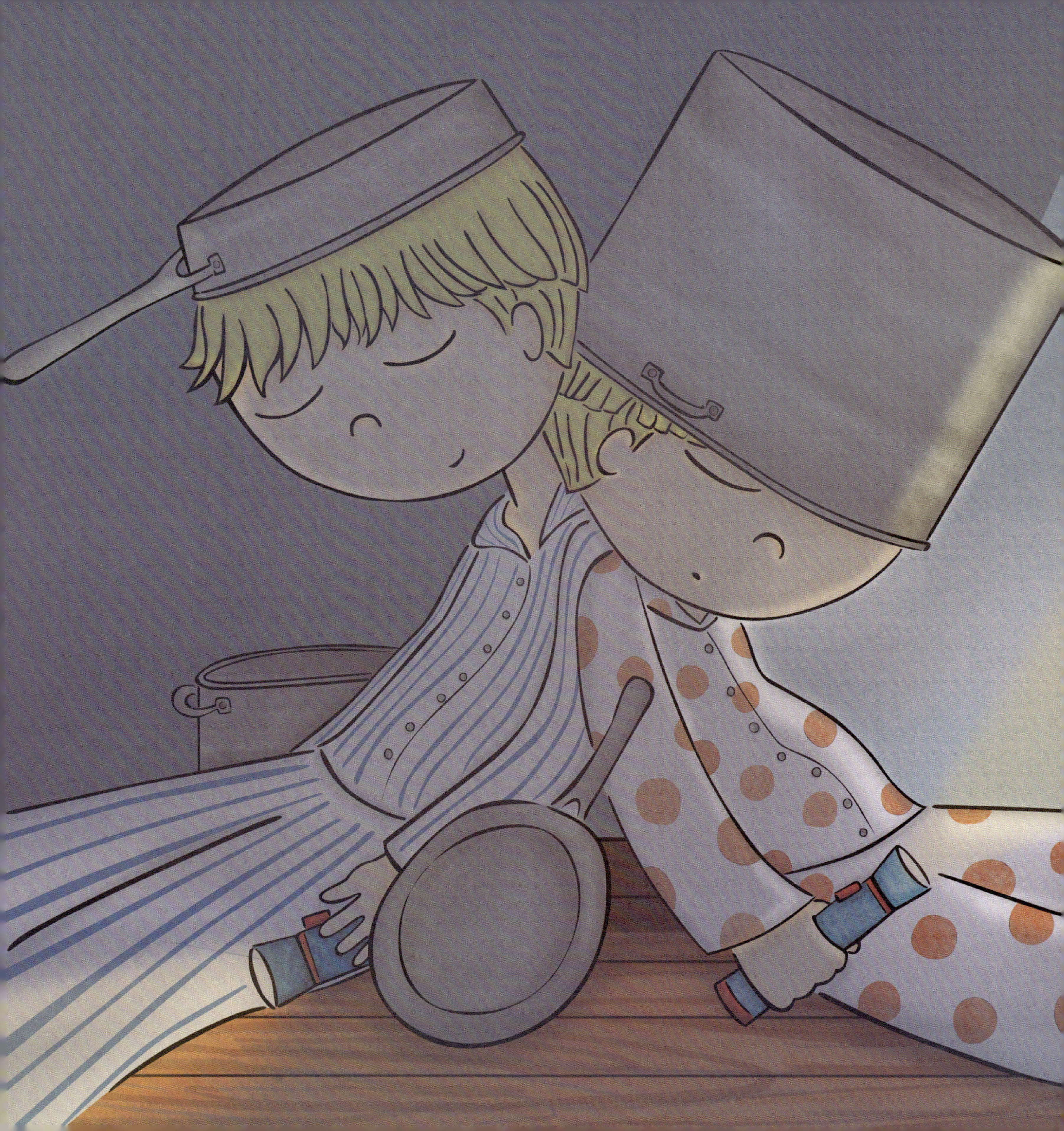

Hours and hours went by. They waited a lot longer this time. They tried really hard to stay awake, but it was long past their bedtime. They just couldn't help it and ended up falling asleep.

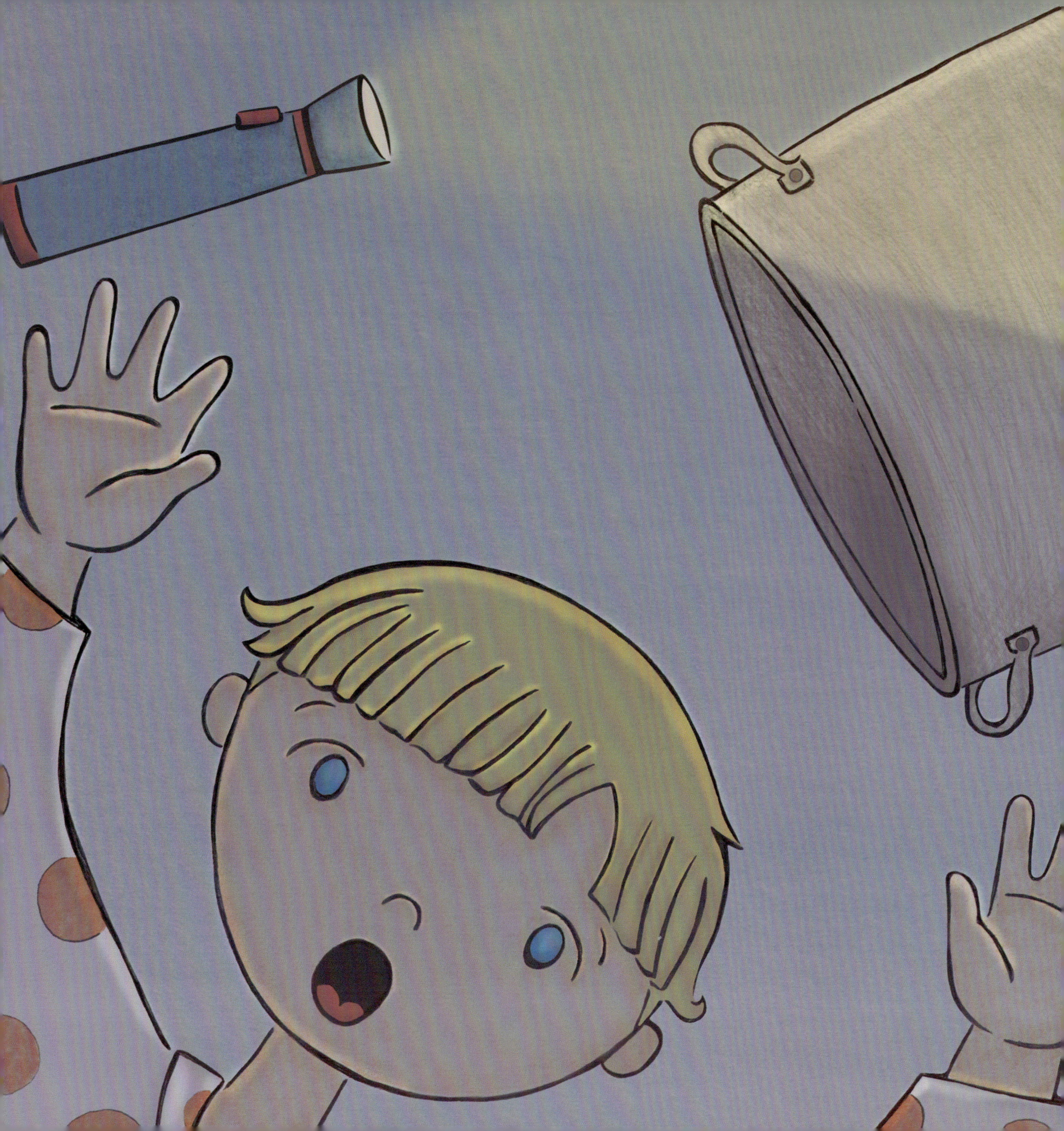

A couple of minutes later, Scott was awakened by a noise. "Squeak, squeak, squeak, squeak." Startled, Scott suddenly jumped and woke up Kevin, who was startled as well. The pot flew off Kevin's head and landed upside down on the floor.

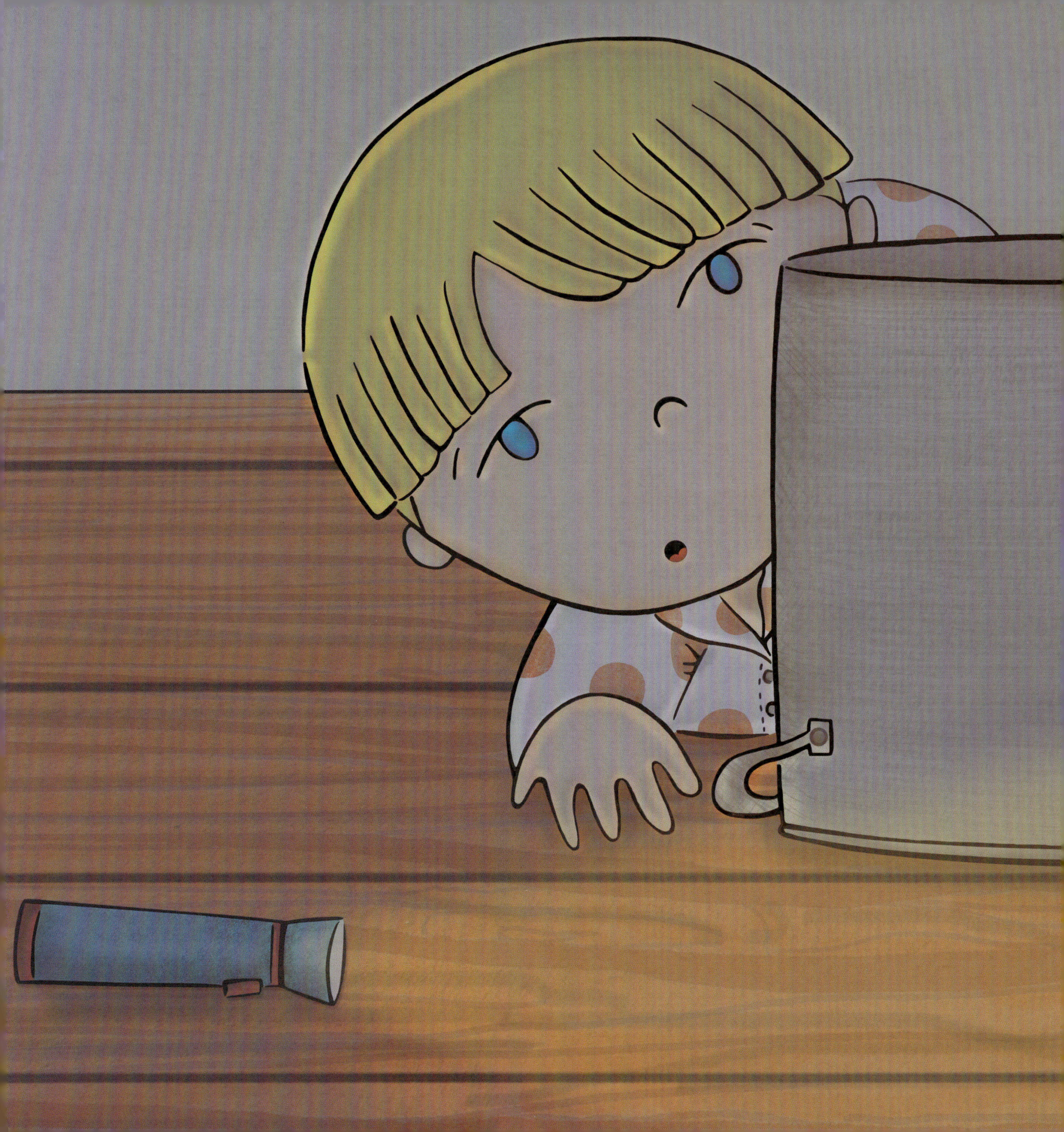

The boys heard a squeaky noise coming from under the pot. They had succeeded! They accidentally caught the culprit! A very squeaky mystery was about to be solved!

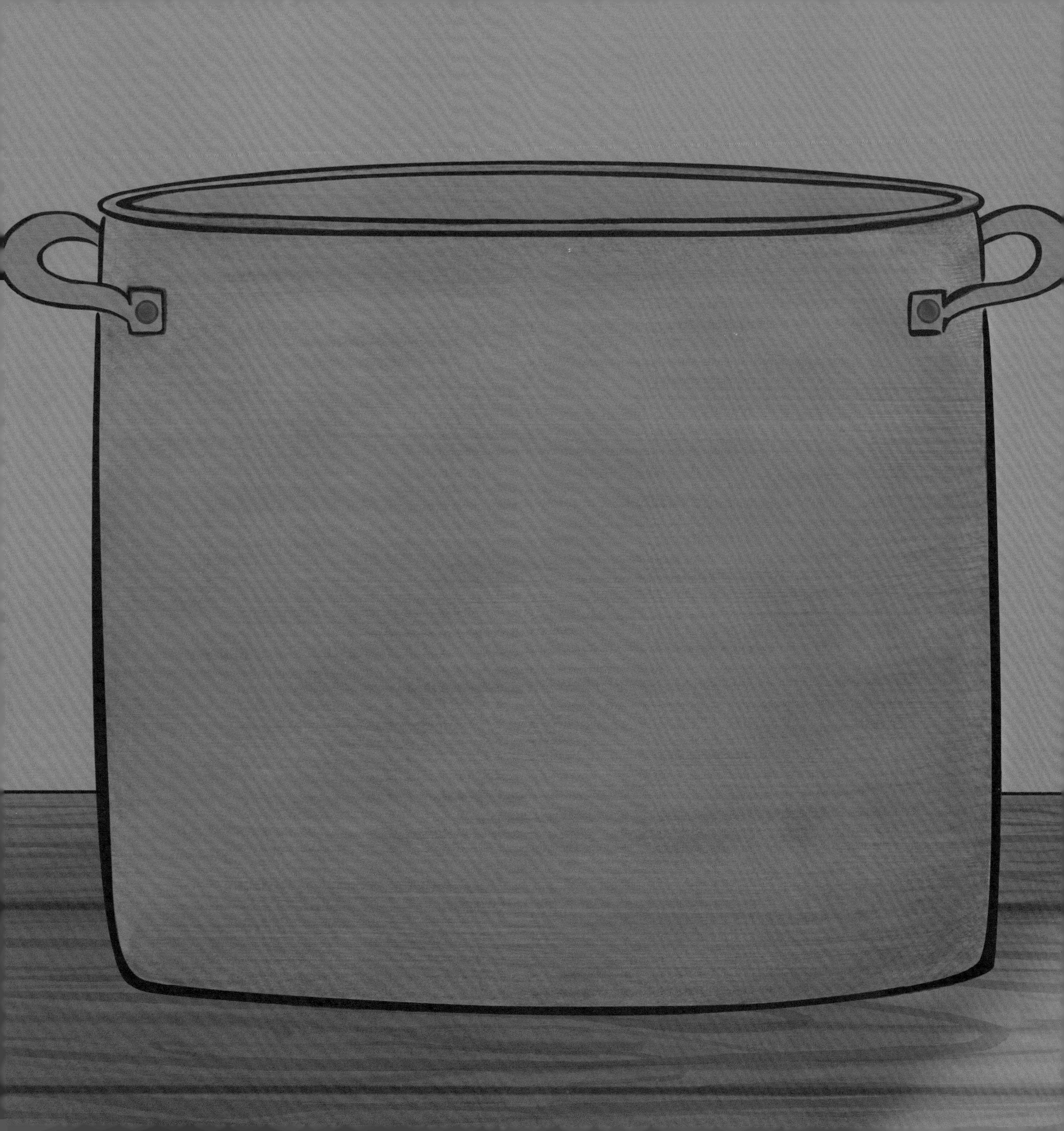

They lifted up the pot to see the squeaky creature. It wasn't a mouse, a bat, or a monster. It was only a tiny green lizard, which did not run away. Instead, it wanted to play and be their friend.

"You seem like a very nice little fellow," said Scott.

"Of course, we can be friends!" added Kevin. "And since you've been a very lucky lizard, that's what we'll name you! Lucky the Lizard."

From that day on, every time the twins stayed at the cabin on vacation, Kevin, Scott, and Lucky the Lizard were inseparable. The twins even built Lucky a tiny bed next to their beds!

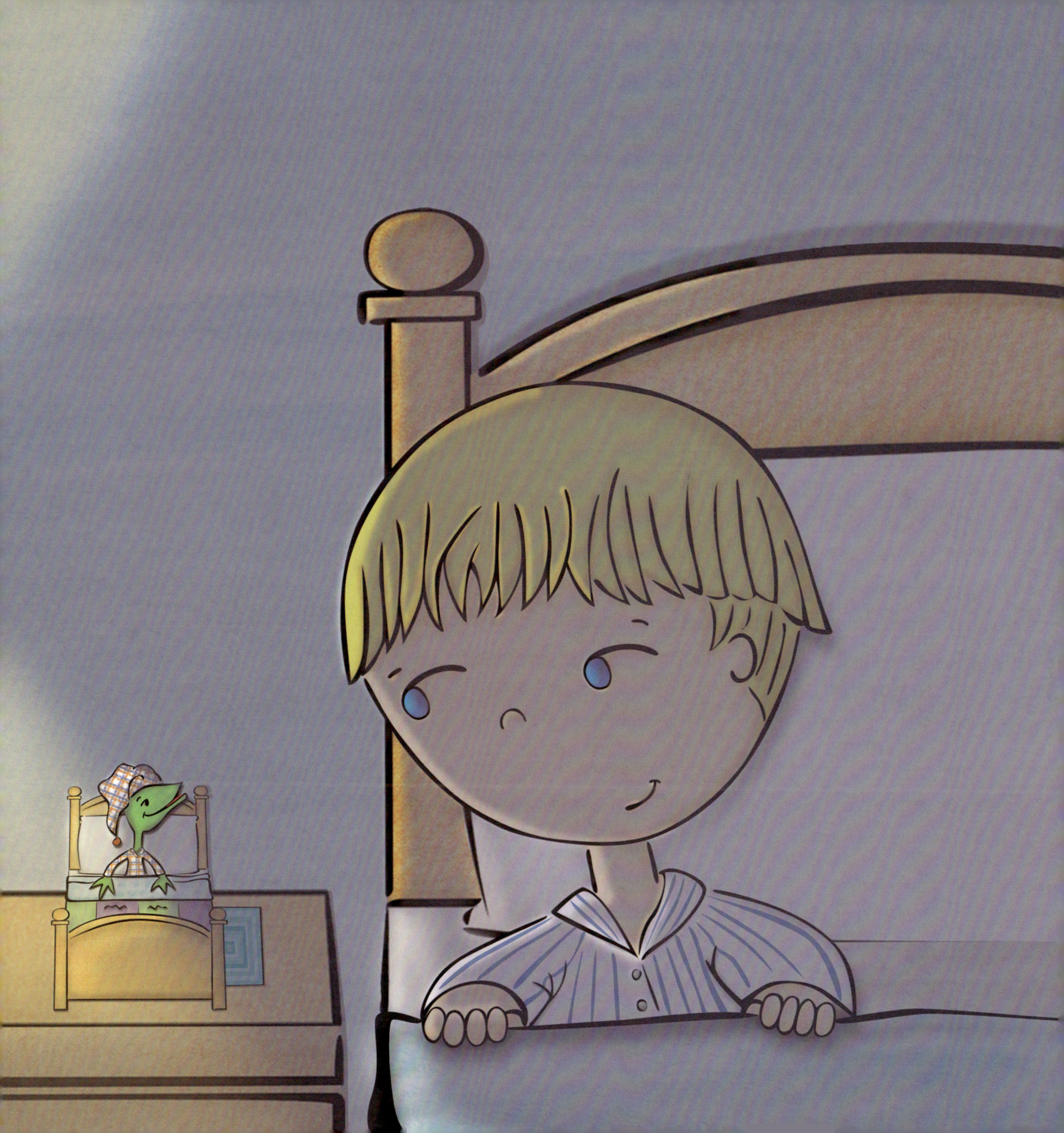

The three of them had lots of fun playing hide and seek, climbing trees and skipping stones in a river nearby. And every afternoon, they shared a yummy peanut butter and jelly sandwich at four o'clock.

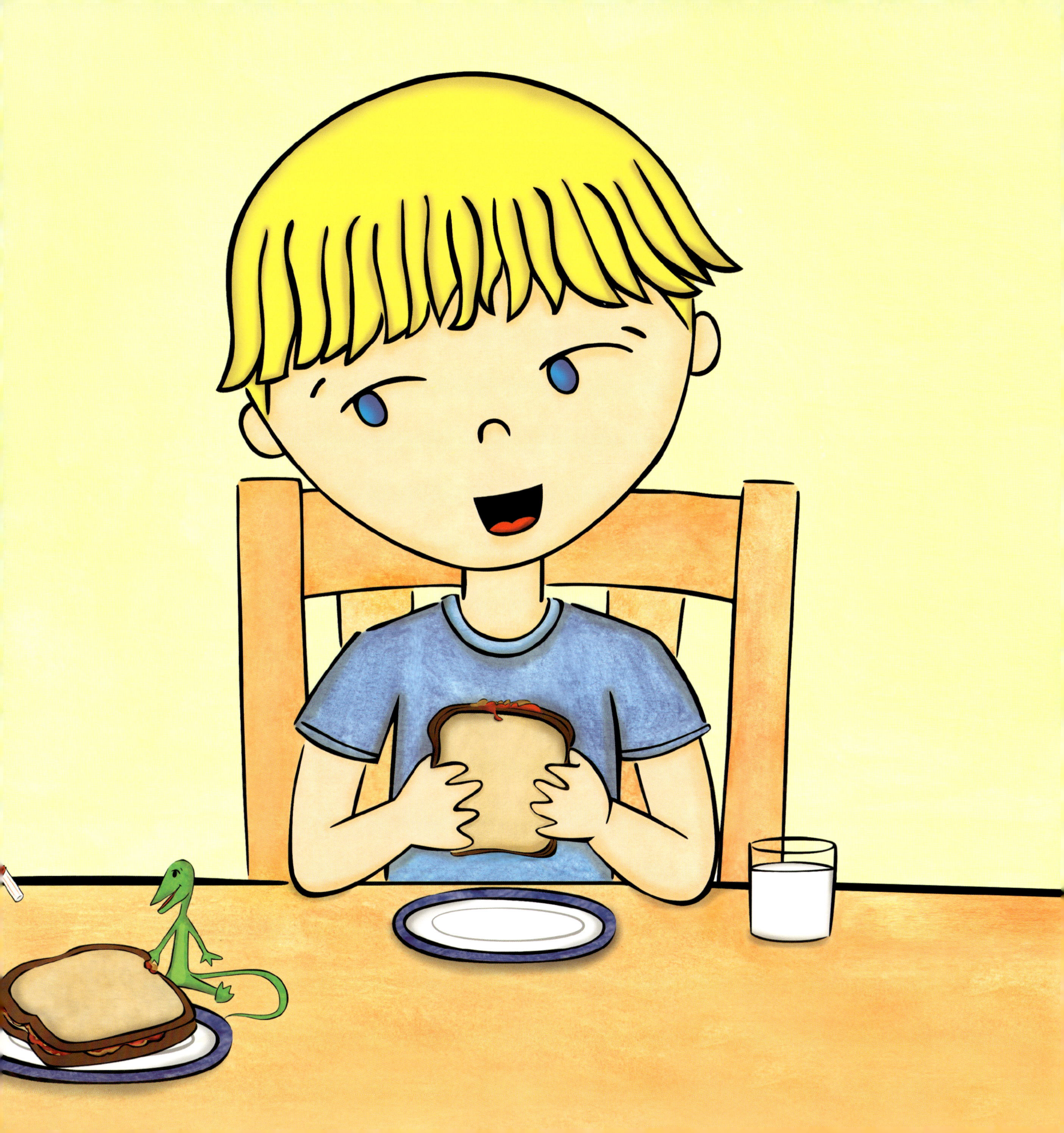

At a local fair

Tower of soup cans

Kevin

Playing the guitar

Thanksgiving Day

Cowboys in pajamas